Bernese Mountain Dogs

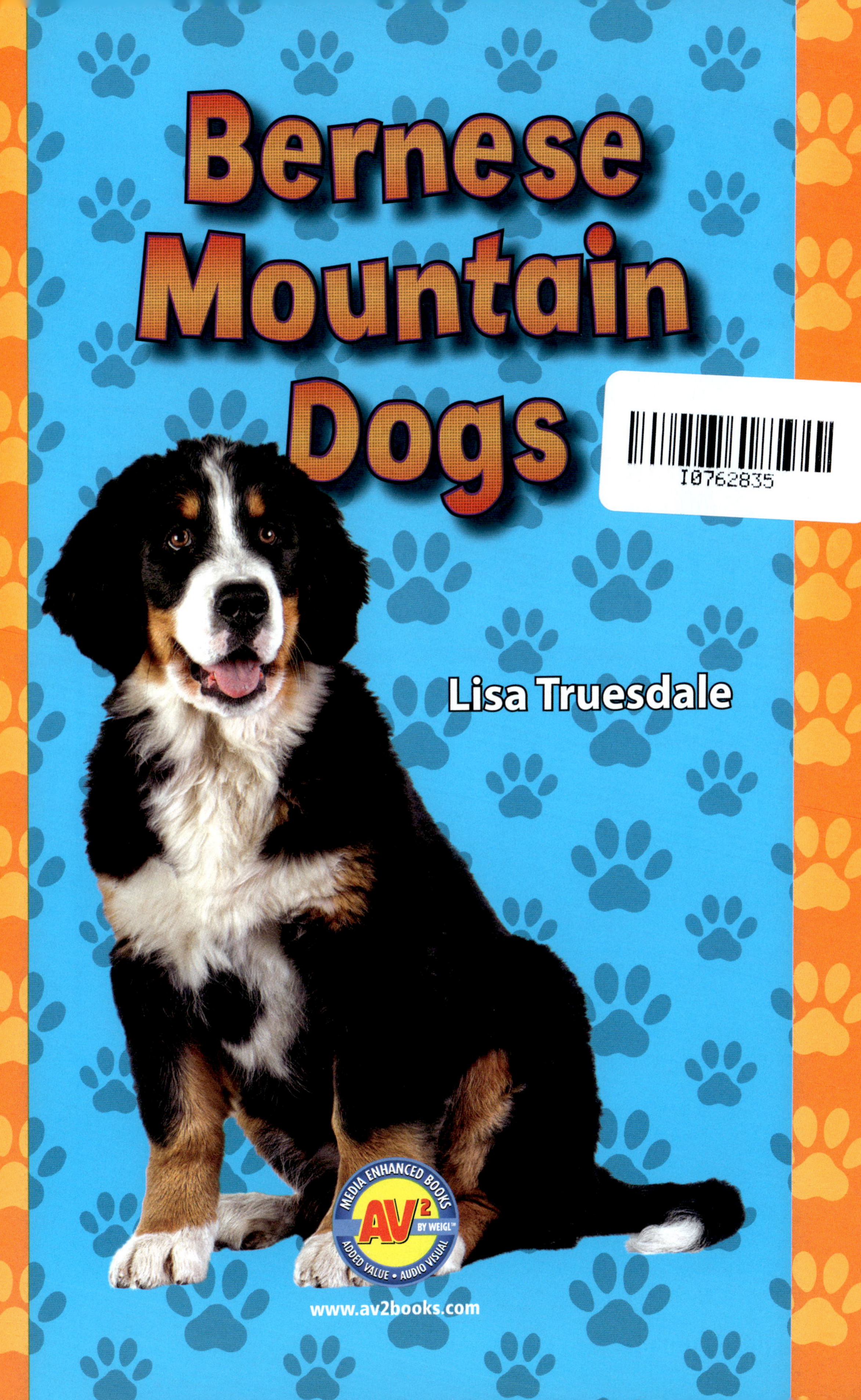

Lisa Truesdale

www.av2books.com

I0762835

Go to www.av2books.com, and enter this book's unique code.

BOOK CODE

LBZ28824

AV² by Weigl brings you media enhanced books that support active learning.

AV² provides enriched content that supplements and complements this book. Weigl's AV² books strive to create inspired learning and engage young minds in a total learning experience.

Your AV² Media Enhanced books come alive with...

Audio
Listen to sections of the book read aloud.

Key Words
Study vocabulary, and complete a matching word activity.

Video
Watch informative video clips.

Quizzes
Test your knowledge.

Embedded Weblinks
Gain additional information for research.

Slide Show
View images and captions, and prepare a presentation.

Try This!
Complete activities and hands-on experiments.

... and much, much more!

Published by AV² by Weigl
350 5th Avenue, 59th Floor
New York, NY 10118
Website: www.av2books.com

Copyright © 2019 AV² by Weigl
All rights reserved. No part of this publication may be reproduced, stored in a retrieval system, or transmitted in any form or by any means, electronic, mechanical, photocopying, recording, or otherwise, without the prior written permission of the publisher.

Library of Congress Control Number: 2017960035

ISBN 978-1-4896-7372-5 (hardcover)
ISBN 978-1-4896-7962-8 (softcover)
ISBN 978-1-4896-7373-2 (multi-user eBook)

Printed in the United States of America in Brainerd, Minnesota
1 2 3 4 5 6 7 8 9 0 22 21 20 19 18

012018
120817

Project Coordinator: John Willis Art Director: Terry Paulhus

Every reasonable effort has been made to trace ownership and to obtain permission to reprint copyright material. The publisher would be pleased to have any errors or omissions brought to its attention so that they may be corrected in subsequent printings.

Weigl acknowledges Getty Images and Alamy as its primary image suppliers for this title.

Bernese Mountain Dogs

Contents

Name That Dog

What strong dog can pull 10 times its weight?

What dog likes to make its owners laugh?

What dog is always three colors?

What dog loves to dig?

Did you guess the Bernese mountain dog?

You are right!

Farm Life

Thousands of years ago, armies from Rome invaded the country of Switzerland. They brought big, hardworking dogs with them. Most people believe that those dogs were the **ancestors** of Bernese mountain dogs.

In Switzerland, Bernese mountain dogs are known as Berner Sennenhunds. They are called "Berners" for short. They are named for the **canton** of Bern, the area of the country where they come from.

Switzerland is a small country in Europe. It is surrounded by France, Germany, Austria, and Italy.
France
Germany
Switzerland
Austria
Italy
Mediterranean Sea

Berners are one of the four types of Swiss mountain dogs. They are the only Swiss mountain dogs to have long, flowing hair. They are also known as Bernese cattle dogs or Swiss cattle dogs. Sometimes, they are called *gelbbacker*. The word means "yellow cheeks."

Berners are very large and smart dogs. In the past, they lived and worked on farms high up in the snowy mountains of Bern. They are so strong that they can pull up to 1,000 pounds (450 kilograms). That is 10 times their weight.

The first known Bernese mountain dog in the United States lived on a farm in Kansas in 1926. The farmer tried to **register** the **breed** with the American **Kennel** Club (AKC). However, the AKC did not accept the breed until 1937.

In 2017, the AKC ranked Berners as the 27th most popular breed of dog in the United States.

Bernese mountain dogs shed their heavy coats twice a year, in the spring and in the fall.

What These Big Dogs Look Like

The Bernese mountain dog is one of the largest dog breeds. Males are 25 to 28 inches (64 to 71 centimeters) tall at the shoulder. They weigh 86 to 110 pounds (39 to 50 kg). Female Berners are a bit smaller than males. They stand about 23 to 26 inches (58 to 66 cm) tall at the shoulder. Females weigh a little bit less than males, too. They weigh 79 to 110 pounds (36 to 50 kg).

Berners have a thick double coat of fur. Their fur is **adapted** to cold weather because they come from the mountains. They have woolly fur underneath and longer fur on top.

The head of a Bernese mountain dog is flat on top, and its nose is wide and straight. They have ears shaped like triangles with rounded tips. Their oval eyes are usually dark brown. Their tail is bushy and wavy.

The medium-length fur of a Bernese mountain dog is **tricolor**. It is mostly jet black with bright white and rust-colored markings. The rust color is over each eye, on the sides of the mouth, and on the sides of the chest. It is also under the tail and on all four legs.

The ends of a Berner's paws are white. It looks like these dogs are wearing little white socks. There is a white horseshoe shape around their nose and up between their eyes. There is also white on their chest. It often makes a shape that is called a "Swiss cross."

While many dogs have brown, pink, or even blue noses, a Bernese mountain dog's nose is black.

The Berner Personality

Bernese mountain dogs are often patient and gentle with children. If a child gets too rough during play, a Berner will usually just walk away. It will not be **aggressive** with the child.

Berners get along with other pets in the house, even cats. They are also comfortable around large farm animals, such as horses and cows. This is because of the farms their ancestors lived on.

Bernese mountain dogs that grow up with children are often particularly confident, friendly, and trusting.

Berners should be exposed to new people and experiences as they grow. This helps them be less shy around strangers.

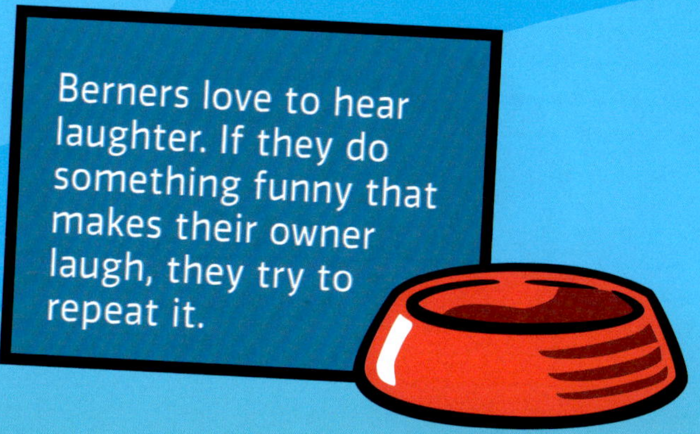

Bernese mountain dogs are big, but they are not big barkers. Berners are pretty quiet. Sometimes, they make a soft growling noise instead of barking.

Most Berners enjoy riding in cars. They enjoy going to places like parks because there are people there. They might be shy when they first meet new people. After that, they are friendly.

Berners stay close to their family. Sometimes, they lean against their owner. This is their own type of hug. They also like to sit on top of their owner's feet. To get attention, they might touch their owner's hand or arm with their nose. This is called a "Berner bump."

Berner Puppies

Bernese mountain dog mothers usually have six to eight puppies in a **litter**. Sometimes, they have only one puppy at a time. They can also have as many as 14 puppies at once, but that does not happen often.

Berner puppies are blind and deaf when they are born. They can see and hear when they are about three weeks old. They usually take their first steps around this same time. Berner puppies can go to live with their new family when they are at least eight weeks old. They should not leave their mother too early.

In their first months, Bernese mountain dog puppies grow between 2 and 4 pounds (1 and 2 kg) each week.

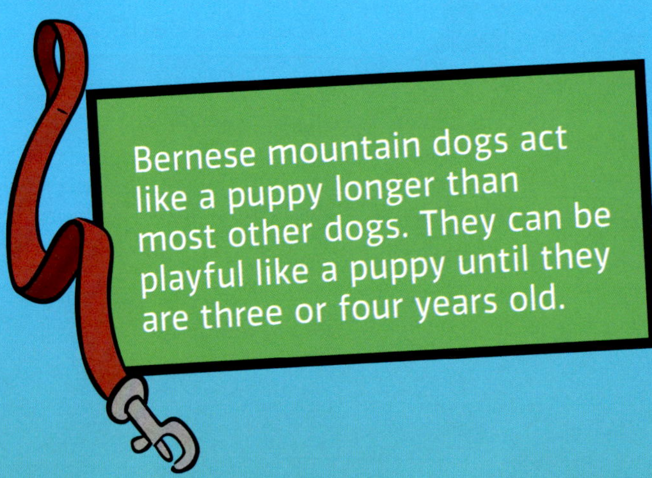

Young Berners may need a special diet to help manage their growth. If Bernese mountain dog puppies grow too quickly, it can hurt their bones. This can also cause problems when they are fully grown.

The area around a Bernese puppy's shoulders is very tender when they are growing. Berner puppies should never be picked up by their front legs or under their shoulders. The best way to pick up a puppy is from underneath.

Bernese puppies need support on their chest and rear when carried. A puppy should be held the same way a small child is held.

Bernese mountain dogs have worked with Swiss farmers for more than 2,000 years. Today, they show their skills at dog shows around the world.

Berners Hard at Work

Back in Switzerland, Bernese mountain dogs worked a lot. They learned to pull carts full of goods. They lived on farms and protected their families and the farm animals. Berners guarded farmhouses and fields. Sometimes, they helped to **herd** cattle or other farm animals. They also pulled carts full of milk, cheese, and vegetables to markets in towns.

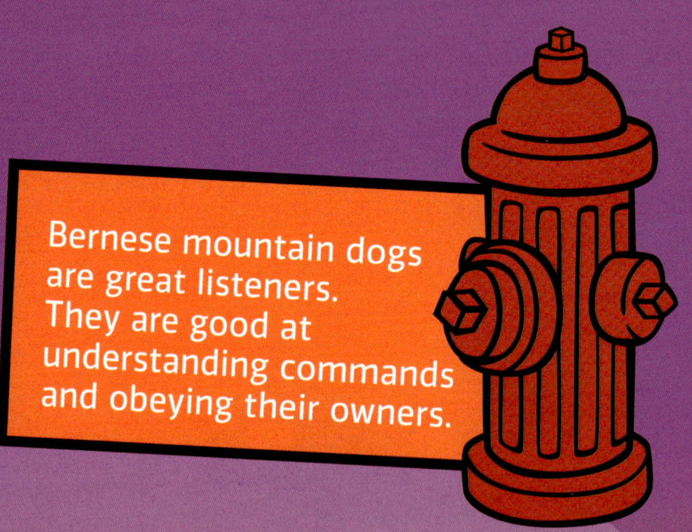

Bernese mountain dogs are still very protective of humans in danger. They can be good watchdogs. Despite being mostly quiet, they will bark to announce strangers. Sometimes, Bernese mountain dogs can help people in dangerous situations. They have been known to save people from drowning and alert people of fires.

Berners still like to work. Their owners can give them little jobs to do. On a hiking trip, a Bernese mountain dog can carry a small backpack with food inside. On a paper route, a Berner can pull the newspapers in a cart.

Some owners like to enter their Berners in dog shows. They also train their dogs for cart pulling and other working **contests**. These dogs are willing to learn and easy to train. They like to please their owners. Berners like to be **praised** when they do their job well.

Bernese mountain dogs should not pull or carry heavy loads until they are at least two years old.

In addition to yard play, Bernese mountain dogs should get 30 to 120 minutes of exercise a day.

Part of the Family

Family is very important to Bernese mountain dogs. They do not like to be left alone for very long. A Berner would not be happy living in a small kennel outside in the yard.

Bernese mountain dogs need a large space to live and play. The fence around the yard does not need to be too tall. These dogs cannot jump very high.

Berners like to run, but they should not exercise too much in hot weather. Their black coat and large size can cause them to get too hot. When it is hot, they should get their exercise in the mornings and evenings when it is cooler.

Berners also love to dig. Their owners can bury a bone or favorite toy for them to dig up in their yard. That way, Berners will not dig up flowers or grass.

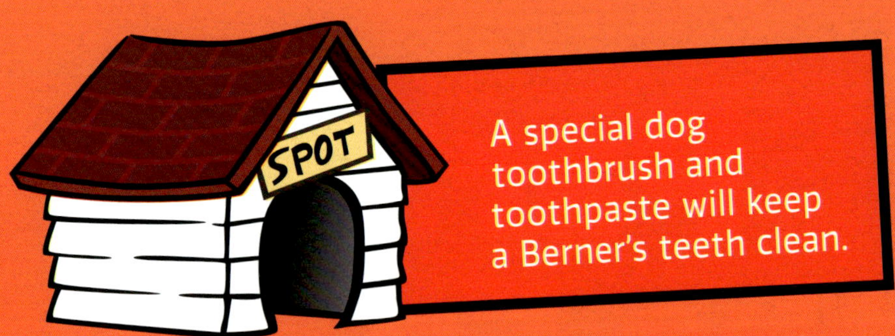

A special dog toothbrush and toothpaste will keep a Berner's teeth clean.

All dogs need care from their owners and regular visits to the veterinarian. Berners shed more than other dogs because their fur is so thick. They have to be brushed often, especially during hot weather. Their nails must also be carefully clipped regularly.

A veterinarian can suggest the right type of dog food for a Berner. Puppies need three or four small meals per day. Older dogs might need only one meal per day, but it is best not to feed them all at once. This could make them sick. Big dogs like Berners often have bone problems when they get older. Their hips and legs might hurt more because of how much they weigh.

With the right care, Bernese mountain dogs live about six to nine years. The oldest living Berner on record was 15 years old. Berners are big and friendly dogs who make their families very happy.

Bernese mountain dogs that are brushed regularly only need to have a bath about twice a year.

Bernese Mountain Dog Quiz

Q: How old was the oldest living Berner?

A: 15

Q: The ends of a Berner's paws are what color?

A: White

Q: Bernese mountain dogs come from which country?

A: Switzerland

Q: How many puppies do most Berner mothers have?

A: Six to eight

Q: Berners can act like a puppy until they are how old?

A: Three or four

Q: What do Bernese mountain dogs love doing in the backyard?

A: Digging

Key Words

adapted (uh-DAPT-ed): to have gotten used to something

aggressive (uh-GRESS-iv): mean or unfriendly, trying to start a fight

ancestors (ANN-sess-turs): people or animals in the same family who lived in the past

breed (BREED): a certain type of an animal

canton (kan-TON): a small territory of a country

contests (KON-tests): events where people or animals try to win by being the best at something

herd (HURD): to gather a group together

kennel (KENN-ul): a crate or small building where owners sometimes put their dogs when they leave the house

litter (LIH-tur): a group of babies born to one animal at the same time

praised (PRAYzd): to be told you did a good job at something

register (REDGE-uh-stur): to keep an official list

tricolor (TRY-kuh-lur): having three colors

Index

Log on to www.av2books.com

AV² by Weigl brings you media enhanced books that support active learning. Go to www.av2books.com, and enter the special code found on page 2 of this book. You will gain access to enriched and enhanced content that supplements and complements this book. Content includes video, audio, weblinks, quizzes, a slide show, and activities.

AV² Online Navigation

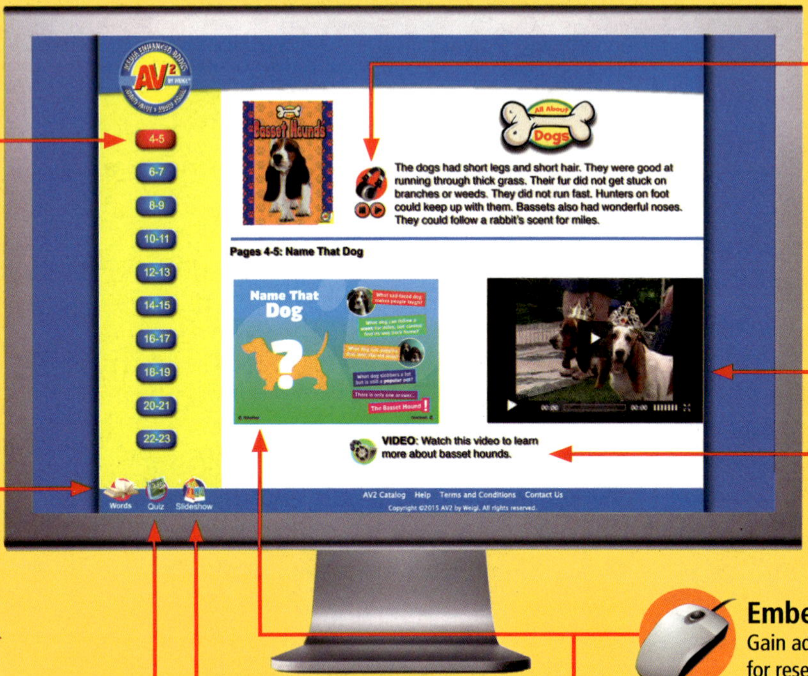

Audio
Listen to sections of the book read aloud.

Book Pages
AV² pages directly correspond to pages in the book.

Video
Watch informative video clips.

Embedded Weblinks
Gain additional information for research.

Key Words
Study vocabulary, and complete a matching word activity.

Try This!
Complete activities and hands-on experiments.

Quizzes
Test your knowledge.

Slide Show
View images and captions, and prepare a presentation.

AV² was built to bridge the gap between print and digital. We encourage you to tell us what you like and what you want to see in the future.

Sign up to be an AV² Ambassador at www.av2books.com/ambassador.

Due to the dynamic nature of the Internet, some of the URLs and activities provided as part of AV² by Weigl may have changed or ceased to exist. AV² by Weigl accepts no responsibility for any such changes. All media enhanced books are regularly monitored to update addresses and sites in a timely manner. Contact AV² by Weigl at 1-866-649-3445 or av2books@weigl.com with any questions, comments, or feedback.